A to Z Animal Mysteries

THE ABSENT ALPACAS

RON ROY'S

A to Z Animal Mysteries™

The Absent Alpacas

WRITTEN BY
KAYLA WHALEY

ILLUSTRATED BY
CHLOE BURGETT

A STEPPING STONE BOOK™

Random House 🏠 New York

Text copyright © 2023 by Kayla Whaley
Cover art and interior illustrations copyright © 2023 by Chloe Burgett
Original A to Z Mysteries® series created by Ron Roy

All rights reserved. Published in the United States by Random House Children's Books, a division of Penguin Random House LLC, New York.

Random House and the colophon and A to Z Mysteries are registered trademarks and A Stepping Stone Book and the colophon and the A to Z Mysteries colophon are trademarks of Penguin Random House LLC.

Visit us on the Web!
rhcbooks.com

Educators and librarians, for a variety of teaching tools, visit us at RHTeachersLibrarians.com

Library of Congress Cataloging-in-Publication Data is available upon request.
ISBN 978-0-593-48899-7 (trade) — ISBN 978-0-593-48900-0 (lib. bdg.) —
ISBN 978-0-593-48901-7 (ebook)

MANUFACTURED IN CHINA
10 9 8 7 6 5 4 3 2 1

This book has been officially leveled by using the F&P Text Level Gradient™ Leveling System.

CHAPTER 1

Abigail "Abbi" Wallace scanned her list one last time.

Sunscreen
Sunglasses
Phone
Money
Alfalfa sprouts

"Check, check, and check," she said. "Okay, I think we're good to go."

"Finally," Abbi's best friend Lydia

Herrera said. "We're gonna miss the start of the costume contest if we don't hurry!"

Lydia sprinted for the mudroom. It was the easiest way in and out of the castle where Abbi lived. Barkley, Abbi's chocolate Bassador (basset hound and Labrador mix), was right on her heels.

Lydia's twin brother and Abbi's *other* best friend, Daniel, rolled his eyes. "Always in such a hurry."

"Wait!" Abbi yelled. "I forgot the most important thing!"

She rushed over to the big kitchen island and pointed. "The tickets! I can't reach them." The marble countertop was just at Abbi's eyeline. She couldn't stretch

her arms up far enough to reach the tickets while in her wheelchair.

Lydia strolled over and handed the tickets to Abbi. Printed in big letters on each were the words *Maine State Fair.* ADMIT ONE.

"*Now* can we go?" Lydia practically whined. Barkley joined in.

Abbi laughed at her friend, while Daniel lovingly shook his head. Abbi stuck the tickets in her pocket and nodded.

"Let's get this show on the road."

—

The fairgrounds weren't far from the castle where Abbi and her adoptive mom, mystery writer Wallis Wallace, lived. But it was certainly too far to go by foot. So Abbi's uncle, Walker Wallace, drove them to the front gate.

"I'm glad we got tickets in advance,"

Abbi said as she got out of the van. "We'd never get through there."

She pointed toward the ticket booth, where a group of people were blocking the path into the fairgrounds. Most had homemade signs that said things like ANIMALS AREN'T AMUSEMENT and ANIMAL RIGHTS RIGHT NOW. One woman with bright-red hair held a megaphone and led the group in chanting similar slogans.

"They're still at it, huh?" Uncle Walker said.

"Who are they?" Abbi asked.

He pressed a button on the key fob, and the van's electric ramp began to fold back up. "Protestors. They think

having the animals in competitions is cruel."

Abbi looked at the small group. "So they don't want the fair to happen?"

"Nah, not the whole fair, just the parts having to do with animals. Sort of like that costume contest y'all are going to."

Walker got back in the driver's seat and rolled down the window. He yelled out, "You kids have fun, now, and don't eat too much funnel cake!"

Abbi raised three fingers in a "Scout's honor" gesture.

Daniel saluted before sticking his hands back in the pockets of his denim overalls.

Lydia grinned and shouted, "No promises, sir!"

It was a beautiful fall morning. The air was as crisp and sweet as a caramel apple. The sky was a bright blue that seemed to go on forever.

Abbi, Lydia, Daniel, and Barkley made their way through the main pathway of the fair. They dodged guests eating cotton candy and men in colorful aprons selling giant soft pretzels. They ignored the flashing lights and *bring-bring* sound effects of the game booths.

The only time they stopped was so Barkley could sniff a fellow four-legged guest. It was a large German shepherd. Abbi considered pulling out her phone to record the yipping sound he made—strange for such a big dog—but there wasn't any time.

They made it to the 4-H pavilion right as the announcer stepped onstage.

Abbi and Lydia glanced giddily at

each other and high-fived. Daniel leaned forward, eager for the show to start.

"Welcome, friends," the host said in a booming voice, "to Maine's very first Alpaca Costume Contest!"

The crowd cheered. Abbi leaned over to the Herrera twins and whispered, "You have to point out which one your mom's friend owns."

"Of course!" Lydia replied.

"We obviously have to root for Alpaca in Wonderland," Daniel agreed.

Abbi giggled at the animal's punny name and held her phone up to record the entire proceeding.

A man, wearing a blue badge with SECURITY printed in bold letters across the front, stepped quickly

onstage. He tapped the host on the shoulder. After a mumbled conversation, the host looked at the audience.

"I'm afraid the contest is being slightly delayed," he said. "Please hold tight, and we'll be back shortly! Thank you for your patience!"

The host followed the security guard and rushed off the stage.

"What was that about?" Daniel asked.

Abbi looked at her friends with the best innocent face she could muster. "Only one way to find out."

"Snooping?" Lydia asked.

Abbi and Daniel nodded. "Snooping."

CHAPTER 2

The barn behind the 4-H pavilion was in shambles. Security guards ran to and fro, trying to calm the angry alpaca owners. And fair workers ran to and fro, trying to calm the animals nervous about their angry owners!

Daniel hopped onto a nearby bench. "Look!" he said, pointing to the far side of the crowd. "There's Ms. Margery!"

They made their way to a tall woman with a concerned look on her face. The woman wore a pink plaid shirt with faded jeans. She was talking to one of the fair staff members.

"Are you sure my Alpaca in Wonderland is safe?" they heard her say. "He's very fragile. Can't even handle fireworks! Oh, he must be so scared."

"Ma'am," the staff member said, "please just wait here while we sort things out." He walked swiftly away and left Ms. Margery wringing her hands with tears in her eyes.

Lydia rushed to her family friend's side. "What happened, Ms. Margery?"

"They're missing! The alpacas are gone!"

Abbi's mouth dropped open, while Daniel and Lydia gasped in unison. Even Barkley let out a startled yip.

"*All* of them?" Daniel asked. "What about Alpaca in Wonderland?"

Ms. Margery wiped her eyes. She took a deep breath. "He's the only one left. He's still safe and sound in his pen, but he must be so scared!"

Abbi opened the Maine State Fair informational booklet they'd gotten at the entrance. She flipped to the alpaca section and ran her finger down the page. "There were twelve alpacas entered

ALPACA COSTUME CONTEST

THIS YEAR'S ALPACAS:

01 AL the pirate
02 Big Baby
03 Super Alpaca
04 ROY. G. BIV.
05 AL-STAR
06 Lumberjalpaca
07 Unicorn Farms
08 Alpaca of Freedom
09 Mario the Alpaca
10 Alpaca in Wonderland
11 Paca Paca Boom Boom
12 Alpaca the Magic Dragon

in the costume contest."

"So if Alpaca in Wonderland is the only one left . . . ," Lydia said.

"Eleven alpacas disappeared into thin air," Abbi confirmed.

Before Ms. Margery could respond, a member of the security team came over. The name tag on her uniform said PATRICIA. "Are you Margery Meadows?" she asked.

"*Ms.* Margery," Lydia corrected sternly. She kept a protective hand on Ms. Margery's arm.

"Ms. Margery," Patricia continued, "we'd like to ask you some questions."

"What kind of questions?" Abbi asked. "Is this an investigation? Is she a suspect?"

The woman laughed. "Now, what

would you kids know about suspects and investigations? This is why you shouldn't watch so much TV."

Abbi tried very hard not to roll her eyes. She mostly succeeded. What this woman didn't know was that her mother was a famous mystery writer. Abbi herself had helped solve a few mysteries with her friends Dink, Josh, and Ruth Rose.

Patricia pulled out a small notepad and a pen. "You own Meadows' Meadows, is that correct?"

Ms. Margery nodded. "Our petting z-anctuary."

Abbi shot a confused look at her friends. Daniel leaned down and whispered, "Part petting zoo;

part animal sanctuary, where injured animals go to recover. Z-anctuary."

Abbi smiled.

"This costume contest comes with a hefty prize," Patricia said. "Might make caring for all those wild animals easier, huh?"

Lydia bristled. She stood on the tiptoes of her black boots. "What's that supposed to mean? You think *Ms. Margery* stole the alpacas?"

Daniel stepped up to Ms. Margery's other side. He and Lydia looked fierce, like knights.

Before Patricia could answer, something that sounded like a big group of particularly upset people crashed toward them. Abbi looked for the commotion. Then she heard a voice over a megaphone recite some familiar slogans. It was the protestors!

Patricia sighed and said, "I have to go deal with this. Don't leave."

Ms. Margery held up her hands. "Wouldn't dream of it."

Once Patricia was gone, Lydia turned to Abbi and lowered her voice. "We're gonna help her, right?"

Abbi nodded. "Looks like we've got eleven missing alpacas to find."

CHAPTER 3

"I can't believe that security lady had the nerve to accuse Ms. Margery!" Lydia said.

Abbi did not say that Patricia never actually accused Ms. Margery. Patricia was just asking questions like any good investigator. Instead, Abbi followed her furious friend toward the pens where the alpacas were last seen: the scene of the maybe-crime. They still didn't even know if the alpacas had been stolen or had only gotten loose. They could be wandering

around right this minute, munching on
wildflowers and waiting to be found.

Abbi hoped that was the case.

"How long have you guys known
her?" Abbi asked.

"Forever!" Lydia said over her shoulder. "Our mom's been volunteering at
Meadows' Meadows since *she* was a kid."

"We used to go almost every week-end," Daniel said. He walked next to Abbi, both of them happy to let Lydia lead the way. "My favorite time to go was in winter, though."

"Why?" Abbi asked.

He thought for a moment. "I guess the animals just seemed really cozy, all huddled up in their pens."

Abbi remembered what Daniel had said about Meadows' Meadows being

a sanctuary. "What kind of animals do they rescue?"

"All kinds!" Lydia called excitedly. "Mountain lions and wolves. Giant snakes. Even peacocks!"

Abbi had never seen any peacocks in real life. Not outside a zoo, where there were too many people and too much noise to get a useful audio recording of them for her collection.

As they got closer to the barn, Lydia asked, "Do you think Security will let us in?"

Abbi smiled. "I think they're too busy to care."

Sure enough, when they arrived at the alpaca barn, there were no staff members to be seen. They must have been called to handle the increasingly rowdy crowds by the pavilion. Even from here, Abbi could hear garbled megaphone sounds from the protest and a mess of overlapping voices.

Everyone was worried about the alpacas. Abbi shook her head. *If only they weren't too busy yelling at each other to actually help find them,* she thought.

"Stay here, Barkley," Abbi said. "Keep a lookout for us, okay?"

Barkley whimpered mildly before lying down on the hard-packed dirt. He was more cuddle-bug than guard dog, but he could certainly make a ruckus when needed. If anyone was about to stumble on them, Barkley would let them know before they could get caught.

As expected, the pens inside were empty.

The silence felt eerie after the noise outside. Abbi's tires crunched loudly over the hay-strewn ground. Whenever

she paused to look inside a pen, the electronic *click* of her motor stopping echoed up to the rafters.

"Look! There's Alpaca in Wonderland!" Lydia said. She rushed to one of the last pens and cooed as she opened the gate. "Hi, buddy. You okay?"

Alpaca in Wonderland looked perfectly happy. He was lying down in a big pile of hay, sleepy-eyed and smiling. He still wore his contest-ready costume. Abbi had expected him to be dressed like his namesake, Alice in Wonderland. But instead, he was dressed as the Queen of Hearts. He even had a crown on his head!

Abbi approached the royal alpaca cautiously. Her wheelchair sometimes spooked animals who weren't used to it, so she gave him plenty of time to watch her.

When she reached him, she took out a handful of the alfalfa sprouts she'd packed. Palm out, she offered the tasty treat to him.

"Oh, don't even bother," Lydia said. "Alpaca in Wonderland *hates* veggies."

"Really?" Abbi asked, pulling her hand back. "I thought alpacas loved them!"

Daniel nodded. "Most do."

"But this one only likes sweet treats," Lydia said. "Sugar cubes, mostly."

Abbi looked around to see if any of the animal handlers had left some sugary snacks lying out. None in here. Maybe somewhere else in the barn? She went back into the main area.

"Hey, look at this," she said.

The twins came out behind her. Daniel closed the gate so Alpaca in Wonderland would stay safe and sound.

"What is it?" Lydia asked.

"Veggies!" Leafy scraps littered the barn floor. The bits of food were just tiny pieces of leaves or stems outside each of the empty pens. Abbi hadn't noticed them before. "It looks like a trail."

Daniel knelt down to get a closer look. He picked up one of the bigger leaves. "It's lettuce."

"Most alpacas love veggies, right?" Abbi said. Daniel nodded.

"But not Alpaca in Wonderland," Lydia said. "He hates them."

"Maybe someone used the lettuce to lure the alpacas away," Abbi said thoughtfully. "But Alpaca in Wonderland didn't fall for it, and that's why he's the only one left!"

Lydia jumped to her feet. "Which proves Ms. Margery didn't have anything to do with it!"

Abbi bit her lip. "Maybe."

Lydia crossed her arms and glared.

"I'm not saying she's involved!" Abbi rushed to say. "We just don't know enough yet to prove anything."

"She's right, Lyddie Bug," Daniel said

gently. His sister stuck her tongue out, but she didn't argue.

Abbi looked around the barn floor again. "It looks like the lettuce trail leads out the back door! Let's follow it."

She turned toward the front door and whistled. "Barkley, come on! We've got a lead, boy!"

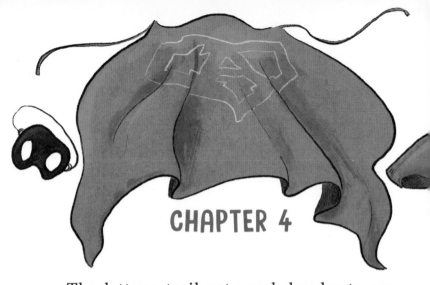

CHAPTER 4

The lettuce trail got much harder to see once they left the barn. The grassy fields leading away from the fair were the same color as the lettuce!

Thankfully, Barkley didn't need to *see* the lettuce to find it.

"Good boy," Abbi encouraged him. "Use that nose. Keep going."

The three friends followed Barkley as he sniffed out the path.

"Since *obviously* Ms. Margery wasn't involved—" Lydia started.

"Probably," Abbi whispered under her breath.

Lydia didn't hear and continued, "Who do you think *did* do it?"

Abbi thought about it. She wondered what her mom would say. What clues would she have seen that Abbi missed? Who would seem suspicious to her? Where would she find a motive?

Abbi wasn't like her mom or her mystery-solving friends from Green Lawn, Connecticut. She liked puzzles, but she wasn't the best at them. She was good with *animals.* Learning about them. Listening to them. Because animals weren't puzzles to be solved. They were creatures to be known.

"I don't know," she finally admitted. "I think we should just focus on finding them first."

Lydia tightened her ponytail. "I think it was the protestors."

"Really?" Daniel asked. "Wouldn't thieves hate having that much attention on them?"

"Come on, you heard how angry they were about the costume contest!"

"That's true," Abbi said, "but I still don't think—"

The trio stopped short. They had reached the edge of the fairgrounds. Beyond the open back gate were a dirt road and woods.

Barkley lay down. There was no more lettuce for him to follow. A dead end.

Lydia sighed in frustration. "Well, what now? Where could they have gone?"

"There must have been a truck waiting here to pick up the alpacas," Abbi guessed.

"Can't we follow the tire tracks, then, or something?" Lydia asked.

Daniel scanned the road. "I doubt it. This road is so full of ruts, I don't think we could tell which tracks were the right ones."

Suddenly Barkley jumped up and started barking. Not his guard dog bark. It was his friendly, excited bark.

Abbi looked toward where he was barking. It was the German shepherd from earlier! The big dog pulled on his leash, tugging his owner to Barkley.

"Hi again!" the woman said. "How are you all enjoying the fair?"

Abbi and Daniel looked at each other, unsure how to answer.

"Um, it's definitely been interesting!" Lydia said.

Barkley and his new friend sniffed each other and exchanged a few licks. The bigger dog looked a bit different, though. He was wearing a cape!

"That's new," Abbi said, pointing to the bright-red fabric. A giant letter *A* was stitched in the center. It looked like the Superman logo but with an *A* instead of an *S*. "Was he wearing a cape earlier?"

The woman laughed. "Isn't it cute? We found it in the woods during our walk. Someone dumped a whole heap of

clothes there. They all looked brand-new, too! We're on our way to report the mess to the park rangers."

Abbi sat up straighter in her chair. "Clothes? Did they look like costumes, maybe?"

"Actually, yeah," the woman said. "Now that you say that, they did!"

The woman pointed them in the direction of the discarded clothing, and Barkley said good-bye to his friend.

Abbi led them toward the woods—and, hopefully, one step closer to the missing alpacas.

CHAPTER 5

"I hope we don't have to go far off the road," Abbi said. "My chair can't drive over anything too rough!"

"Or too soft," Lydia said. "Remember when you tried to follow that seagull at the beach and got stuck in the sand?"

"I didn't know the sand was that loose!" Abbi said, laughing. "Uncle Walker made the funniest noises trying to pull me out."

"He squawked more than the seagulls did!" Lydia imitated the sound.

Daniel nudged her shoulder, laughing. "Hey, he was doing his best!"

"I should have recorded *him* for my sound collection instead," Abbi said.

They reached the edge of the woods. Soft grass turned into hard dirt and tree roots.

"Don't worry," Lydia said, serious now. "We'll make sure you don't get stuck this time."

The three friends made their way through the trees carefully. The ground was definitely bumpier here. Lydia and Daniel moved the bigger rocks and fallen branches that occasionally blocked Abbi's way. But mostly it was smooth sailing.

Soon the trees opened up into a little clearing.

"Look!" Lydia cried. She ran over to a pile of fabric and started rummaging through it. She held up an alpaca-size pirate hat.

"Think it would look good on Barkley?" she asked.

He gave a sharp bark as if to say "Don't even think about it."

"These are the costumes, all right," Daniel said. He fished a sparkly rainbow ribbon from the pile. Abbi held up her wrist expectantly and smiled as he tied the ribbon on to her.

"So what do we know?" Abbi asked. "Someone used lettuce to lead away all the alpacas—"

"Except Alpaca in Wonderland!" Lydia clarified.

"All the alpacas except him," Abbi confirmed. "They probably loaded them up in some sort of truck and drove a little ways down the road."

"Then they must have taken off all the costumes and left them here," Daniel said. He gestured to the oversized baby bonnet his sister had tied on to her head. "You think the alpacas waited in the truck?"

Abbi nodded. "There's no way the kidnappers would

have made eleven alpacas trek through the woods. Why bother?"

"Okaaaaay, so . . . what now?" Lydia asked. "Where would they go next?"

Abbi bit her lip.

The trail had gone cold.

—

The walk out of the woods seemed even longer than before. Abbi couldn't shake the feeling of failure. Lydia looked as down as Abbi felt.

"We did everything we could," Daniel said. "And hey! Maybe someone found them while we were gone!"

Abbi tried to smile. "Maybe."

They were nearly back to the road when Barkley jerked his head upward.

His ears pricked up, too. "What's wrong, buddy?" Abbi asked.

Just then, a loud, strange sound echoed through the woods.

"What was *that*?" Lydia asked.

Abbi cocked her head, listening intently. The sound came again. Loud, like a chimpanzee. But melodic, like a bird.

48

"That's way too loud to be any song-bird," Abbi said to herself.

"It's a bird?" Lydia said. She gasped. "It *is* a bird! That sounds like one of Ms. Margery's peacocks!"

"Lydia, where is Meadows' Meadows? Are we close by?"

Lydia looked around, lost. "Um, maybe?"

"Yeah, I think we are," Daniel said, excited. "I didn't remember earlier, but it's pretty close to the fairgrounds!"

Barkley whined as the peacock's call sounded again.

"I can't think of a better place to hide a herd of stolen alpacas than a z-anctuary, can you?" Abbi asked.

CHAPTER 6

Lydia looked angry. "Are they trying to frame Ms. Margery?" She looked as if she might storm off.

Abbi grabbed her friend's sleeve before she could take another step. "We don't even know if that's where they are! Let's just go have a look first."

Lydia took a long, calming breath. "Fine. No jumping to conclusions. But if this *is* a frame job, I'll make sure those kidnappers regret it!"

She held up her fists as if ready to fight.

Abbi and Daniel laughed. Lydia wouldn't hurt a fly. Literally! Whenever a fly got in the house, she would carefully catch it and let it go outside.

"You look ridiculous," Abbi said, still giggling. "Come on, let's follow that peacock call before it stops singing!"

Meadows' Meadows was even closer than they'd thought. Within ten minutes, they had found the entrance.

"It's been a while since we've been here," Lydia said. "Mom hasn't taken us to volunteer as much as usual."

"Why not?" Abbi asked.

Lydia shrugged. "No reason. Just busy, I guess. I miss it, though."

"Me too," Daniel said.

Abbi looked around for the peacock. She wanted to record that sound it was making!

"There's the main barn," Lydia said. "Let's check there first."

They headed toward the main barn, where the petting-zoo animals lived. When the farm was open to visitors, many of the sheep and bunnies and alpacas would be out on the gated front lawn. But now the farm was closed, so all the animals stayed cozy near their private barn.

Lydia and Daniel raced off to inspect the barn. Abbi took her time getting there, making sure to look for clues.

Just then, the peacock sound stopped for a moment, and Abbi heard something else. A long, low humming sound. Almost like a cow's moo but softer. It was the same sound Alpaca in Wonderland had made earlier! She turned toward the noise.

"We found them!" Lydia shouted at the same time. "Over here!"

Sure enough, a small herd of alpacas were grazing in the field next to the barn.

Lydia took off, too excited to wait. Abbi called out, "No, don't run! We don't want to scare them."

Lydia stopped and nodded.

"Always in such a hurry!" Daniel said, just as he had that morning.

The three friends approached slowly.

"Do these look like Ms. Margery's usual alpacas?" Abbi asked.

Lydia considered. She looked at each of them in turn. "I can't tell. I don't remember there being this many, but again, it's been a while since we've come here. What do you think, Daniel?"

"There definitely weren't this many before," he said. "But maybe they got more since our last visit?"

When Abbi reached the fence, she pulled out her bag of alfalfa sprouts. She cautiously put her hand through the

slats. The closest alpaca sniffed the treats but didn't eat any.

"It's okay, buddy," Abbi said softly. "Want something yummy?"

"Doubt they're too hungry," a deep, friendly voice called from behind them. "They had a big breakfast."

Abbi startled and dropped the sprouts.

A man was walking toward them from the direction of Ms. Margery's house. He looked around the age of Abbi's mom, but his hair was already graying.

"Mr. Stevie!" Lydia said. "You're Ms. Margery's son, right? I remember you from when we were little."

The man smiled. "That's me."

"I thought you moved to Oregon," Daniel said.

Mr. Stevie stuck his hands in his pockets. "I moved back here this past year to help Mom out on the farm. Money's been tight lately."

"It has?" Lydia asked, surprised.

He looked away. "Ah, well, you know. Attendance has been down. Guess not as many people want to trek out here when there are so many things to do in town."

The twins nodded. An awkward silence fell on the group.

Mr. Stevie reached down to pet Barkley, but the Bassador slid closer to Abbi. She patted his head reassuringly.

"Well, I hate to be the bearer of bad news," he said, "but we're closed today on account of the fair and all."

"Are these Ms. Margery's alpacas?" Abbi asked. She figured there was no use hemming and hawing, as Uncle Walker would say. Better to get to the point.

Mr. Stevie tilted his head. "Sorry?"

"We just came from the fair," she explained. "There's a bunch of alpacas missing."

After half a beat, he laughed. "And you think these are them? Nah, these guys have been here for ages." He turned to Lydia. "You probably remember most of them, huh? If you've been coming here for so long."

Lydia looked at her brother. "Um, yeah, I definitely remember *some* alpacas."

"Well, there's your answer!" Mr. Stevie said. "Now, let's get you kids back to the festivities, shall we?"

He started to walk away, but Abbi didn't move.

"Aren't you worried about Alpaca in Wonderland?" she asked.

He paused and turned. "Pardon?"

"Ms. Margery's entry for the costume contest. I just said a bunch of the alpacas were missing, but you aren't worried?"

Mr. Stevie pulled his hands from his

pockets. Little pieces of paper and gum wrappers fell out. He crossed his arms.

"Of course I am! That alpaca's our pride and joy," he said. "I would head back with you to look for him, but I'm not sure I'll be able to get a ticket. And someone has to stay here with the animals, you know."

Abbi locked eyes with him, still refusing to move.

"You definitely weren't at the fair this morning?" Daniel asked.

The man scoffed. "Nope. Been here all day." He turned and strolled toward the front gate.

Daniel knelt down and picked up one of the pieces of paper Mr. Stevie had dropped. On it was a picture of a Ferris wheel with today's date stamped in red ink. Daniel handed it to Abbi and asked quietly, "Then why does he have a torn ticket stub?"

Abbi's eyes darted to the ripped paper. It was identical to the ones in their own pockets. Which meant Mr. Stevie was lying. And Abbi wanted to know why.

CHAPTER 7

Lydia whipped out her phone and typed a quick text. She showed Abbi the screen. Abbi gave her a thumbs-up.

"Excuse me, sir?" Abbi called out.

Mr. Stevie turned back toward them. He was smiling again. But he seemed nervous, too. "Come along, kids. I gotta feed the sheep once I see you off."

Abbi pointed at the feet of the alpaca she had tried to feed earlier. Its nails were painted the exact same rainbow shades as the ribbon tied around her wrist.

"Did Ms. Margery paint these nails?" she asked. "Was she gonna enter this alpaca in the costume contest instead of Alpaca in Wonderland?"

Mr. Stevie's face paled. "Oh, uh, we thought we were allowed to enter two different alpacas. But turns out we read the rules wrong." He laughed. It sounded

faker than the other times he'd laughed. "Can't win 'em all, right?"

Abbi thought back to what Patricia had said to Ms. Margery: "This costume contest comes with a hefty prize."

Then Abbi thought about what Mr. Stevie had said: "Money's been tight lately."

She felt a hunch deep in her belly. She ran with it.

"It's a shame no one'll get to win now," she said.

He snapped his head toward Abbi. "What d'you mean?"

"Well, with the alpacas missing, they can't exactly

crown a winner, can they? That's what the staff at the fair said, right, Lydia?"

"Right!" Lydia said. "That's exactly what they said!"

Daniel nodded, catching on. "They'll probably have to cancel the whole event."

"They can't do that! Not after every-thing! We *need* that money," Mr. Stevie yelled. "Alpaca in Wonderland should win! He's the only one left. Of course he should win!"

Abbi made her voice as innocent as possible. "How did you know he was the only one left? I don't think we ever said that. Did we, guys?"

Lydia quickly shook her head. Her dark-brown curls bounced around her shoulders. "We sure didn't, Abbi."

The trio stared at Mr. Stevie. He stared at them, too, from Abbi to Lydia to Daniel down to Barkley and back again.

"No?" Mr. Stevie said. He was clearly sweating. "I think you probably did. Yeah, you did."

Abbi inched closer to him. Slowly, so as not to spook him.

"Why did you do it, Mr. Stevie?" Abbi asked in a gentle, low voice. "Why did you take the alpacas?"

CHAPTER 8

Abbi worried Ms. Margery's son might try to run once he realized he'd been caught. Instead, his face crumpled. He fell to a squat and held his head in his hands.

"We need the money," Mr. Stevie said through tears. "Mom doesn't want to admit it, but the farm's failing."

"It's *failing*?" Lydia squealed. "Like it's gonna close down?"

He nodded.

"Maybe, yeah. It's why I moved back home. I thought if Mom had some extra help, maybe we could . . . But we failed. I failed."

Mr. Stevie sniffled and looked up at the concerned faces watching him. "When I saw the prize money they were offering for the costume contest, I knew it would help. Maybe we could hold on long enough to find a solution."

"But you knew there'd be a lot of other alpacas wanting to win, too," Abbi said, putting the pieces together.

He stood up again and looked past Abbi to the alpacas gathered behind them. "I knew Alpaca in Wonderland

wouldn't bother following me if I had veggies. It was easy to make sure he was the only one left."

Lydia crossed her arms. Her angry face was back.

Daniel put a comforting hand on his twin's shoulder. "Your mom almost took the blame, you know," he said. "They thought *she'd* stolen them."

Somehow Mr. Stevie's face turned even whiter. "No. I didn't mean for it to . . . I only wanted to help!"

"Stevie Ashley Meadows!" Ms. Margery's voice was even louder than the peacock's.

She stormed toward them, holding her phone up to her ear. Two of the State Fair staff followed behind her.

Lydia showed her own phone screen to Mr. Stevie. "I called her a while ago," Lydia said. "She heard everything."

"Everything?" Mr. Stevie whispered.

Lydia nodded. "Afraid so."

As Ms. Margery

came ever closer, her son stood. He brushed off his pants. "Guess it's time to face the music. Sorry for getting you kids involved."

Abbi handed him her bag of alfalfa sprouts. "Here. You can make it up to the alpacas, at least, while they're waiting for their rides home."

She looked at her friends and smiled. "Speaking of, let's go find Uncle Walker. I think I've had enough of the fair for one day."

CHAPTER 9

Two months later, on a cool and clear October night, Abbi, Lydia, Daniel, and Barkley were on their way to Meadows' Meadows once again—this time, on a much happier mission.

"Do you think a lot of people will show up?" Lydia asked. "Oh, I'm so nervous!"

Abbi patted her friend's hand. "Don't worry. It's gonna be great."

From the driver's seat, Uncle Walker said, "Everybody's been looking forward

to this shindig. You kids really did something good here."

It had been Lydia's idea to try to
help the farm. It had been Daniel's idea
to throw a Halloween fundraiser. It had
been Abbi's to stage another costume
contest as the main event.

The other alpaca farmers had heard
about Ms. Margery's money troubles by
then, and they were eager to help. Their
enthusiasm for the plan was a huge
relief. Abbi had been worried they might
hold a grudge against Mr. Stevie or even
Ms. Margery. But thankfully, everyone
wanted what was best for the alpacas *and*
for Meadows' Meadows.

Abbi smiled widely as they got out
of the car. The whole farm was deco-

rated! Twinkly fairy lights were draped all around. Dozens of jack-o'-lanterns dotted the grounds. There were even rubber bats swooping down from the barn's eaves! A whole flock of them!

Barkley and Uncle Walker strolled toward the food trucks in the parking lot while Abbi, Daniel, and Lydia headed toward the house.

"Over here, kids!" Ms. Margery called from near the field where the three friends had found the missing alpacas.

Those alpacas were grazing again. But this time, they were all in costume!

"Cuuuute!" Lydia cried as she ran over to the fence. The closest alpaca—dressed as a pirate—sniffed Lydia's outstretched hand, looking for treats. Daniel followed his sister at a much more leisurely pace, but his smile was just as bright as hers.

Mr. Stevie walked up beside Abbi. "Want to feed them?" he asked, holding out a basket of carrots chopped into bite-size pieces.

Abbi smiled and took a bag from the basket, then drove to the fence.

People were wandering around and milling about.

They all seemed to be enjoying the festivities. A few families were petting the sheep. Their wool had been dyed to make them look like other animals! There were zebra stripes, cheetah spots, and tiger stripes.

Other people were bobbing for apples on the front porch. A few were taking pictures of the peacocks lounging like royalty near the main entrance.

Mr. Stevie cleared his throat. "I just wanna thank you kids again for . . . well, for stopping me back then. I messed up, and I'm truly sorry for bringing y'all into the whole mess."

Ms. Margery linked arms with her son. "You

sure did mess up," she said. "But you set things to rights. I think everyone sees you're trying to make amends."

Abbi smiled at the warmth in Ms. Margery's voice. She reached into the basket of carrots and picked a perfectly round slice. She extended her hand toward the nearest alpaca. An astronaut alpaca!

Lydia rushed over and grabbed the carrot out of her hand. "Don't be silly! Alpaca in Wonderland would never *dream* of eating a carrot."

Abbi gasped at the creature wearing the space suit. "This is Alpaca in Wonderland? I didn't recognize him!"

Mr. Stevie laughed. "He couldn't

repeat the same costume twice, could he?
He's Alpaca in Aerospace tonight."

The alpaca looked toward the sky,
as if searching for his next destination
among the stars. But when Ms. Margery

pulled out a sugar cube, his gaze turned back to Earth.

Abbi looked fondly at the alpaca with the sweet tooth. "You know, something tells me he's gonna win this time, for real."

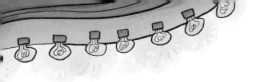

ALPACA FACTS FROM A TO Z!

- *Best-friend material!* Alpacas are social animals, which means they like making friends. It's easy for them to be friends with other farm animals!

- Did you know that alpacas can be different colors? From white to dark gray, alpacas come in twenty-two hues!

- The word for a baby alpaca is *cria.* Aw!

- All alpacas are *domesticated,* which means none live in the wild. They are all raised and live among people.

- Alpaca fur (called *fleece*) is durable—it's both water- and fire-resistant.

- A *llapaca* is a cross between a llama and an alpaca.

- Alpacas can spit up to ten feet! But don't worry—they only do so when annoyed or threatened.

- Alpacas can live to be twenty-five years old. *Wow!*

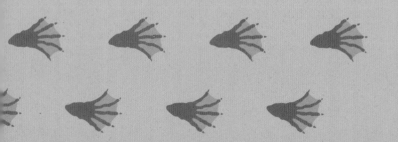

Follow the tracks to the next book!

A TO Z Animal MYSTERIES™

BATS IN THE CASTLE

HAVE YOU READ ALL THE BOOKS IN THE

A to Z Mysteries®

SERIES?

Help Dink, Josh, and Ruth Rose . . .